A little bit
DIFFERENT

Claire Alexander

words & pictures

Here are the Ploofers.

They are going to do something very special,
all together.

They have been practising...

They will do it at the same time...

READY, STEADY...

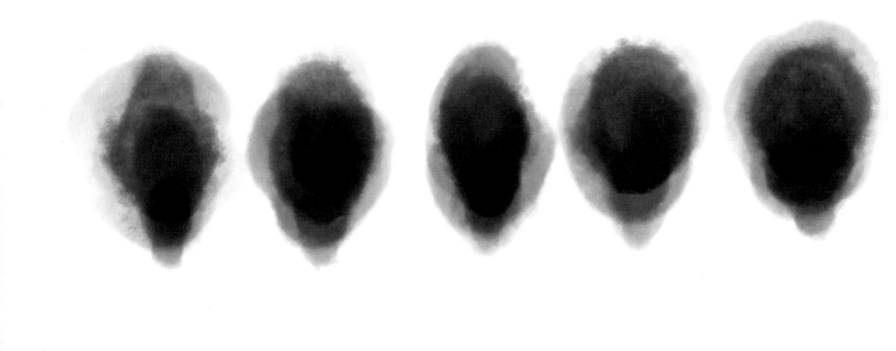

Wow!

Cool!

Awesome!

Brilliant!

Mega!

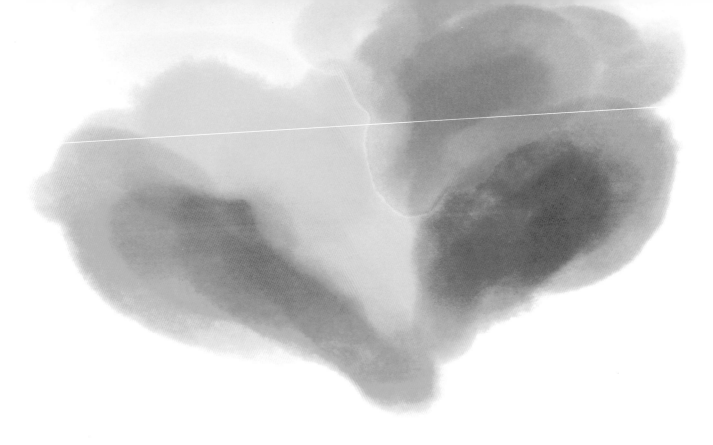

I don't know, but

I LOVE IT!

BUT IT'S DIFFERENT!

Well, it is different!

I don't like it...

It's WEIRD!

Let's go!

They didn't like it.

Why didn't they like it?

WOW!
Did you make that?

It's
beautiful!

Do you think so?

Yes! It's BIG and BRIGHT and COLOURFUL, and SO DIFFERENT!

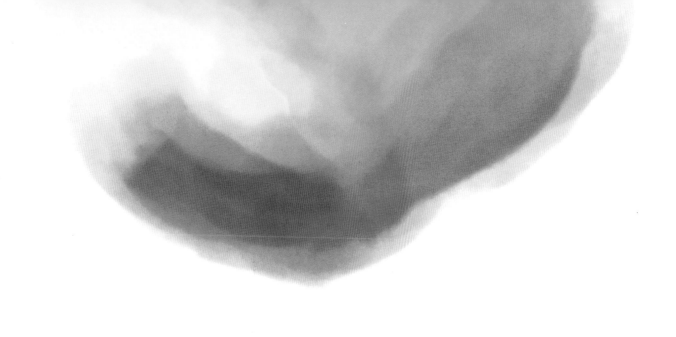

It IS different!

Can you do
it again?

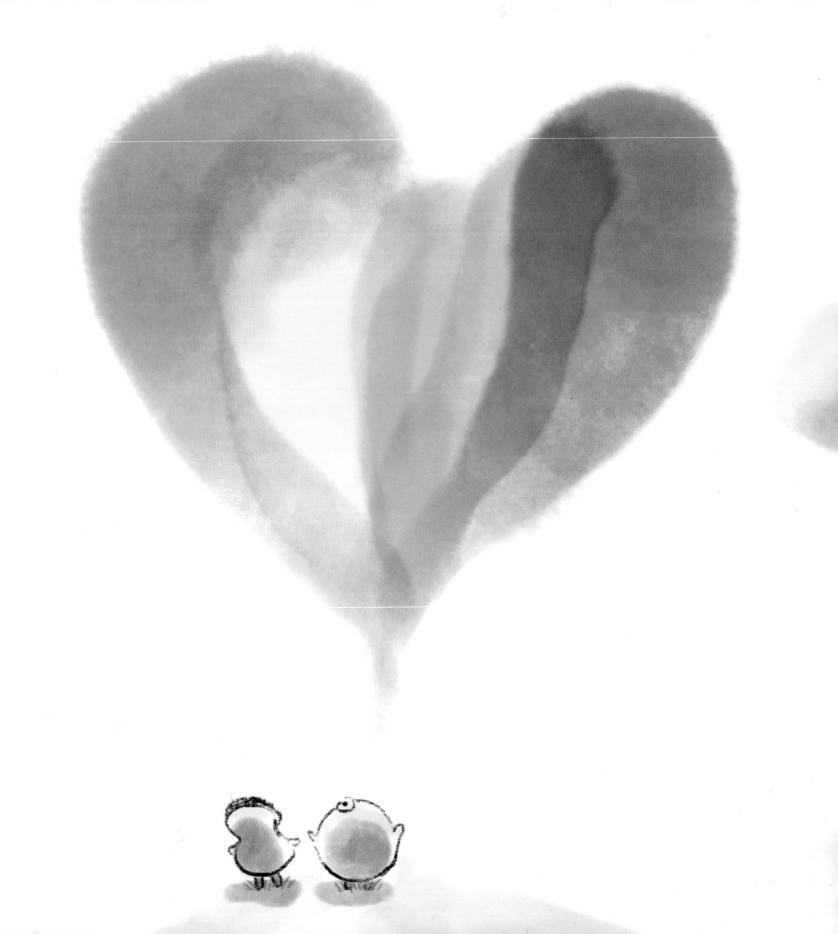

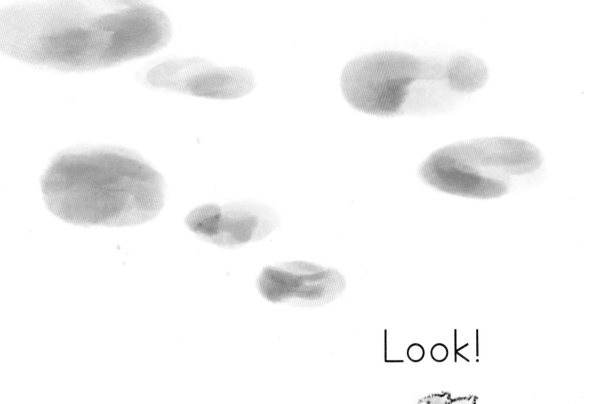

Look!

Aren't they
AMAZING?

They are quite special...

They REALLY are SPECIAL!

Let's all **SHOOF** like you!

READY, STEADY...

For Jodie and Jo

Quarto is the authority on a wide range of topics.
Quarto educates, entertains and enriches the lives of
our readers—enthusiasts and lovers of hands-on living.
www.quartoknows.com

© 2019 Quarto Publishing plc
Text © Claire Alexander
Illustrations © Claire Alexander

Claire Alexander has asserted her right to be identified
as the author and illustrator of this work.

First published in 2019 by words & pictures,
an imprint of The Quarto Group.
The Old Brewery, 6 Blundell Street,
London N7 9BH, United Kingdom.
T (0)20 7700 6700 F (0)20 7700 8066
www.quartoknows.com

A catalogue record for this book is available from the British Library.

ISBN: 978 0 71124 545 7

9 8 7 6 5 4 3 2

Manufactured in Guangdong, China CC112019